Danger in the Forest

First published in 2009
by Wayland

This paperback edition published in 2010 by Wayland

Text copyright © Penny Dolan 2009
Illustration copyright © Kirsten Richards 2009

Wayland
338 Euston Road
London NW1 3BH

Wayland Australia
Level 17/207 Kent Street
Sydney, NSW 2000

Series Editor: Louise John
Editor: Katie Powell
Cover design: Paul Cherrill
Design: D.R.ink
Consultant: Shirley Bickler

A CIP catalogue record for this book is available from the British Library.

ISBN 9780750257404 (hbk)
ISBN 9780750260350 (pbk)

Printed in China

Wayland is a division of Hachette Children's Books,
an Hachette UK Company

www.hachette.co.uk

Danger in the Forest

Written by Penny Dolan
Illustrated by Kirsten Richards

WAYLAND

It was morning and the family sat eating breakfast in their camp.

The sun shone on the leaves of the trees, lighting up the forest around them.

"Children, would you go into the forest and pick some berries for dinner tonight?" Grandpa asked.

"Yes, Grandpa," Erg and Luli answered.

"Remember to keep quiet and watch out for danger," Grandpa said.

Luli and Erg waved goodbye and set off into the forest.

"Listen to the leaves rustling," said Erg.

"Grandpa says that different trees make different sounds," Luli said.

The children walked through the forest until Erg saw some wild berries.

"I recognise these!" cried Erg. "Grandpa told me the red ones are safe to eat."

"Let's take them back to camp," said Luli.

The children wrapped the berries up in leaves and put them in their pouches.

After a while, Erg and Luli stopped
to rest on a patch of grass.

"I'm hungry!" said Erg, stuffing his mouth full of berries.

"Oh, Erg, your lips are stained bright red!" said Luli, laughing loudly.

Suddenly, a gigantic boar burst out of the bushes. His long body was covered in thick bristly hair. He had two huge curling tusks and beady black eyes. He stared fiercely at the children.

"Quick, run!" shouted Erg.

Luli and Erg raced to a big tree and
clambered up the trunk as fast as
they could.

"What are we going to do now? We're trapped," grumbled Erg. "It's your fault for laughing loudly. Grandpa said we're supposed to be quiet in the forest."

"It's your fault for making me laugh," Luli answered grumpily.

Below the tree the boar roamed
backwards and forwards, snorting
at the children.

Soon enough, the boar forgot about Luli and Erg and started to dig up acorns in the earth beneath the tree.

"I'm getting cold," whispered Erg, "and hungry."

"What if we're trapped up here until night time?" asked Luli. "I'm scared."

"Ssh! Did you hear that noise?" asked Erg.

"Yahhh!" cried lots of voices all at once.

Pa, Grandpa and the uncles came rushing out of the trees and charged at the boar. It squealed in terror and ran off into the forest.

"You can come down now," Pa called to Luli and Erg.

When the children were safely on the ground, they hugged Pa tightly.

"Come on, let's go back to camp," Pa said.

"Wait!" said Luli. "Can you hear that buzzing?"

"Bees have made a nest in the tree trunk," said Erg.

"And bees mean honeycomb!" said Pa. "We'll come back later. Grandpa will know the best way to get the honeycomb out."

Luli held up her pouch. "Look how many berries we collected for dinner, Pa!"

Back at camp the children gave Ma the
berries, and told her all about the boar
and the bees.

Pa and Grandpa lit some branches
from the fire.

"The smoke will make the bees sleepy,"
Grandpa explained. "Then we can
get the honeycomb out without
being stung."

"And we'll try and catch that boar, too!" said Pa.

So, Pa, Grandpa and the uncles set off into the forest once again.

Erg and Luli sat by the fire.

"I hope Pa catches that boar," said Luli.
"I'm starving!"

"Me, too!" said Erg.

At last the men returned, carrying the
boar above their heads. Grandpa walked
with them, carrying an enormous basket
full of honeycomb.

That night, there was roast boar,
berries and sweet honeycomb
for dinner.

"What a feast!" said Erg.

"Yes," laughed Luli. "And there's enough to last for days and days!"

START READING is a series of highly enjoyable books for beginner readers. **The books have been carefully graded to match the Book Bands widely used in schools.** This enables readers to be sure they choose books that match their own reading ability.

Look out for the Band colour on the book in our Start Reading logo.

The Bands are:

Pink Band 1A & 1B

Red Band 2

Yellow Band 3

Blue Band 4

Green Band 5

Orange Band 6

Turquoise Band 7

Purple Band 8

Gold Band 9

START READING books can be read independently or shared with an adult. They promote the enjoyment of reading through satisfying stories supported by fun illustrations.

Penny Dolan enjoys writing stories on her computer at home, and sharing stories with children in schools and libraries. Penny also likes reading, painting and playing djembe drums. She has two grown-up children and one bad cat.

Kirsten Richards lives in a small house near Oxford with her two cats, three plants and more spiders than she'd like to contemplate. When freed from her duties of cat food opener and chin scratcher, she draws and paints to her heart's content.